The baby-sitter came.

“Go back to bed,” said Dad.

The children came downstairs.

"We couldn't sleep," they said.

Kipper got his books.

He wanted a story.

Biff was hungry.

They made a sandwich.

Chip wanted a pillow fight.

Everyone joined in.

The children went back to bed.

“What a mess!” said the baby-sitter.

Mum and Dad came back.

“Was everyone good?”
said Mum.

“Yes and no,” said the baby-sitter.